NAUGHTY GEORGE

JANE PILGRIM

Illustrated by F. Stocks May

DERRYDALE BOOKS
New York

George the Kitten lived at
Blackberry Farm with Mr. and Mrs.
Smiles, their children Joy and
Bob, and lots of friendly farm
animals. He was a very bouncy
black-and-white kitten, but he
was not always a very good
kitten, and then he was called
Naughty George.

Sometimes at bedtime Mrs. Smiles could not find George to put him to bed in his little basket beside the kitchen fire, but when she went upstairs he was curled up asleep on Bob's bed. "Naughty George!" she scolded, and gave him to Mr. Smiles to take back to the kitchen.

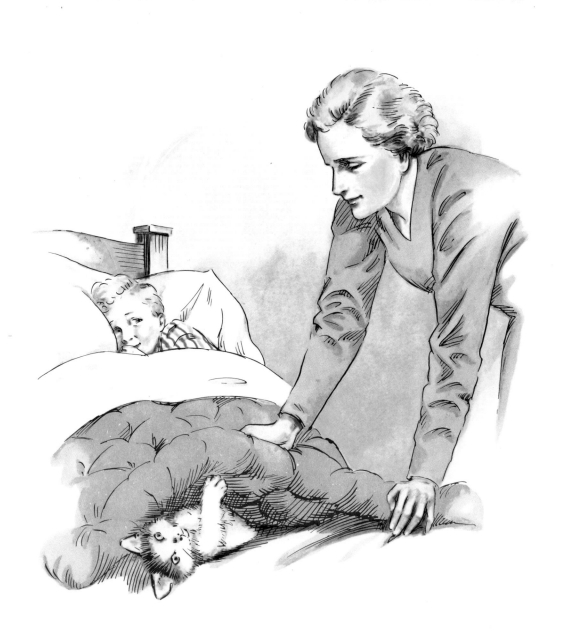

One morning Joy found him on the kitchen table dipping his paw into the cream jug. "Naughty, naughty George!" she cried, and shooed him out into the yard.

It was a lovely sunny morning, and George stretched himself happily and thought how good the cream had tasted. Across the yard he saw the hutch where Bob's tame rabbit lived. "Poor Blue Bun," thought George. "She must be lonely. I'll go and talk to her."

"Good morning, Blue Bun," he said politely. "Would you like to come for a run in the fields with me? It is a lovely morning, and it must be very dull in your hutch."

"Thank you very much, George,"
she said, "but I cannot open my
door." So George jumped onto the
top of the hutch and, leaning over,
pushed the latch with his paw.
The door swung open.

Blue Bun hopped excitedly out
and was soon following George
toward the gate into the field.

But whom should they see coming through the gate but Bob, with Rusty the Sheep Dog! George was alarmed and scampered very quickly up on the wall and watched Bob pick up Blue Bun. "You mustn't run away, Blue Bun," said Bob gently as he stroked her ears. "However did you get out?" And he carried her back to her hutch and carefully shut the door.

George jumped down from the wall and rubbed himself against Rusty's legs. "I let her out, Rusty," he purred. "I thought it was so dull for her in her old hutch." "You are naughty!" scolded Rusty. "Blue Bun might have gotten lost." And then, to show that he wasn't really cross, he played a bouncing game with George all around the yard until they were both tired out.

After that, George lay down in the sunshine on the step outside the kitchen door and slept until dinner time.

Joy brought him out his dinner—a lovely plate of fish—and he began to eat it hungrily. Then Mother Hen and her chick Mary hopped up and tried to take some bits off his plate. George spat fiercely, but they took no notice. He spat again, but they pecked on happily.

Suddenly George shot out a paw
and swatted Mother Hen hard.
"Go away, go away!" he mewed.
"It's my dinner, not yours. Go
away!" And he chased her right
across the yard.

Mr. Smiles heard Mother Hen's squawks as she fled across the yard, and saw George chasing her. "Georgie, Georgie!" he shouted. "Stop that at once!" And he caught George and put him up on his shoulder. "Naughty George," he said, and then he saw little Mary still pecking at the remains of George's dinner. "Poor Georgie," he said, and walked back into the house with George still on his shoulder.

"Here is a very naughty kitten," said Mr. Smiles, and he dumped George in Joy's lap. "He sleeps on our beds, he steals the cream, he lets out the rabbit, and he chases the hens. But I think you should give him a saucer of milk and tell him he is a very sweet kitten as well."

So Joy gave George some milk and
whispered in his furry ear, "You
naughty, darling Georgie, how we
love you!" And George purred
happily and snuggled down in
his basket in the kitchen at
Blackberry Farm.

Text copyright MCMLII by Jane Pilgrim
Illustrations copyright MCMLII by Hodder & Stoughton Ltd
All rights reserved.

This 1987 edition is published by Derrydale Books,
distributed by Crown Publishers, Inc., 225 Park Avenue South, New York,
New York 10003, by arrangement with Hodder & Stoughton Limited

Manufactured in Spain

LIBRARY OF CONGRESS CATALOGING-IN-PUBLICATION DATA

Pilgrim, Jane.
Naughty George / Jane Pilgrim: illustrated by F. Stocks May.
p.   cm.—(Blackberry Farm book series)

Summary: Naughty George, a kitten at Blackberry Farm, gets into
mischief but is lovable anyway.
ISBN 0-517-64348-0
[1. Cats—Fiction.]   I. May, F. Stocks. ill.   II. Title.
III. Series: Pilgrim. Jane. Blackberry Farm book series.
PZ7.P6295Nau   1987

[E]—dc19   87-30303
                                                          CIP
                                                          AC

h g f e d c b a